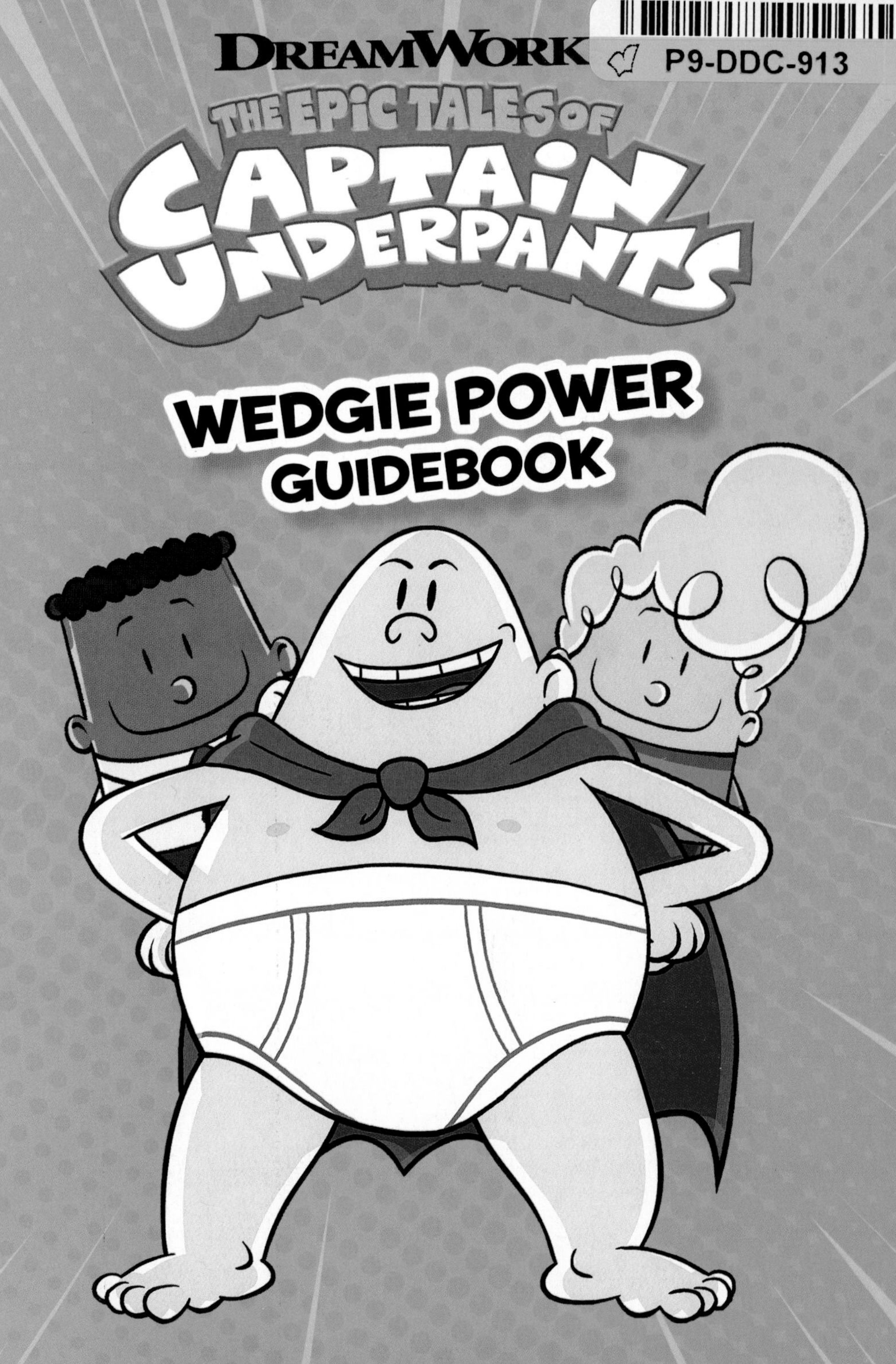
DreamWorks
THE EPIC TALES OF
CAPTAIN UNDERPANTS
WEDGIE POWER
GUIDEBOOK
ADAPTED BY KATE HOWARD

SCHOLASTIC INC.

Photos © Shutterstock: 8 bottom (ogieurvil), 10 background (Mavadee), 14 background and throughout (vectorplus), 17 blobs (MSSA), 19 burst and throughout (Artem Musaev), 25 bottom burst and throughout (Jo ritchy), 45 shorts (Rvector).

ISBN 978-1-338-26921-5

10 9 8 7 6 5 4 3 2 1 18 19 20 21 22

Printed in the U.S.A. 40

Designed by Erin McMahon

First printing 2018

CONTENTS

Chapter One: MEET GEORGE AND HAROLD 4

Chapter Two: GEORGE AND HAROLD'S GREATEST PRANKS 7

Chapter Three: MEAN OLD MR. KRUPP 12

Chapter Four: TREE HOUSE COMIX, INC. 18

Chapter Five: THE ORIGIN OF CAPTAIN UNDERPANTS 26

Chapter Six: MELVIN SNEEDLY AND HIS INVENTIONS 32

Chapter Seven: THE ZANY KIDS OF JEROME HORWITZ ELEMENTARY 38

Chapter Eight: THE STRANGE STAFF OF JEROME HORWITZ ELEMENTARY 43

Chapter Nine: TREE HOUSE COMIX PRESENTS ITS GREATEST HITS 51

Chapter Ten: CAPTAIN UNDERPANTS'S GREATEST BATTLES OF ALL TIME!! 95

Chapter Eleven: GEORGE AND HAROLD'S CREATE-A-COMIC 112

CHAPTER ONE:
MEET GEORGE and HAROLD
George
Harold

THIS IS GEORGE BEARD AND HAROLD HUTCHINS. GEORGE IS THE KID ON THE LEFT WITH THE TIE AND THE FLATTOP. HAROLD IS THE ONE ON THE RIGHT WITH THE T-SHIRT AND THE BAD HAIRCUT. REMEMBER THAT NOW.

THESE TWO PRANKSTERS ARE BEST FRIENDS AND NEIGHBORS. THEY ARE ALSO FOURTH GRADERS AT JEROME HORWITZ ELEMENTARY SCHOOL, HOME OF THE PURPLE DRAGON SING-A-LONG FRIENDS, WHERE YOU MIGHT HEAR THEM DESCRIBED AS:

DISRUPTIVE!
BAD-
ATTITUDED!

BUT THEY ARE ACTUALLY SMART AND SWEET . . . AND A BIT SILLY.

THEIR SILLINESS GETS THEM INTO A LOT OF TROUBLE WITH THE SCHOOL PRINCIPAL,
MR. KRUPP.
HOPE DIES HERE

SOMETIMES, THE MISCHIEF THESE TWO MAKE LEADS TO BIG TROUBLE. BUT BEFORE I CAN TELL YOU THAT STORY, I HAVE TO TELL YOU *THIS* STORY . . .

CHAPTER TWO: GEORGE and HAROLD'S GREATEST PRANKS

GEORGE AND HAROLD *LOVE* PRANKS. SOMETIMES, THEIR JOKES ARE HARMLESS. BUT SOMETIMES, THEIR PRANKS HAVE UNEXPECTED CONSEQUENCES . . . LIKE MAKING GIANT, CRANKY VEGGIES ATTACK THE SCHOOL. BUT THAT'S A STORY FOR ANOTHER TIME

GEORGE AND HAROLD HAVE DONE SOME REALLY SILLY STUFF DURING THEIR TIME AT JEROME HORWITZ ELEMENTARY.

LIKE THAT TIME THEY TOILET-PAPERED PRINCIPAL KRUPP'S CAR.

Jerome Horwitz Elementary
TP! IT'S NOT JUST FOR TUSHIES! IT CAN ALSO BE FOR PRANKS! AND IT'S REALLY A *GAAAAS*!
Jerome Horwitz Elementary
REFRAIN FROM SMILING!
THAT'S GAS AS IN FUNNY. NOT GAS AS IN FARTY! CUZ PRANKING WITH TP IS ALWAYS A BLAST!
NO ONE LOVES TP MORE THAN GEORGE AND HAROLD. NOT FOR ITS INTENDED USE, BUT FOR PRANKS. GEORGE AND HAROLD HAVE SUCCESSFULLY TP'D MOST ITEMS IN THEIR HOMETOWN, PIQUA. BUT THEY'VE ALWAYS HAD THEIR EYES ON AN EVEN BIGGER PRIZE.

TP'ING THE ENTIRE SCHOOL IS GONNA BE THE GREATEST PRANK EVER.
WE'RE GONNA BE LEGENDS.

THEN THERE WAS THE TIME THEY USED THEIR

MY HAMMY SOUND MACHINE

TO HAVE SOME FUN WITH PRINCIPAL KRUPP'S MORNING ANNOUNCEMENTS.

THE MY HAMMY SOUND MACHINE:
created for one purpose—FUN!
IT'S THE MY HAMMY SOUND MACHINE.
IT MAKES OVER TWO THOUSAND AMAZING SOUNDS!
MOOOOOOO!

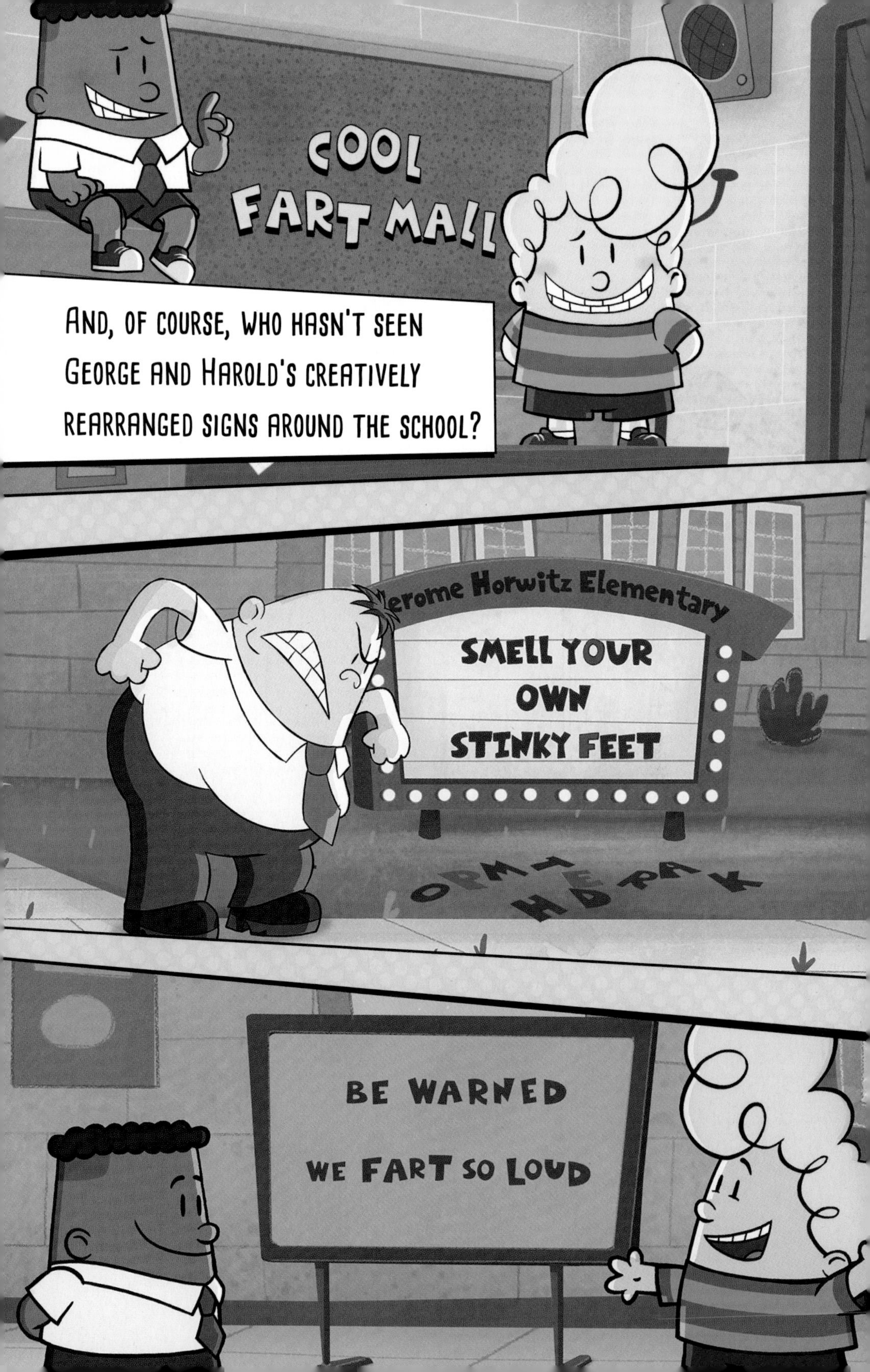
COOL FART MALL
AND, OF COURSE, WHO HASN'T SEEN GEORGE AND HAROLD'S CREATIVELY REARRANGED SIGNS AROUND THE SCHOOL?
Jerome Horwitz Elementary
SMELL YOUR OWN STINKY FEET
BE WARNED
WE FART SO LOUD

CHAPTER THREE: MEAN OLD MR. KRUPP

THE GOAL IS ZERO FUN, PEOPLE! ZERO.
HOPE DIES HERE

THIS IS MEAN OLD MR. KRUPP, THE MEANEST PRINCIPAL IN THE WORLD. MR. KRUPP DISLIKES KIDS . . . AND FUN. SO HE REALLY DISLIKES GEORGE AND HAROLD.

TWO TIGERS TAKE TURNS TASTING TAPIOCA. TWO TIGERS TAKE TURNS TASTING TAPIOCA.
KRUPP
I AM A MOUNTAIN! HOOGA!

EVERY TIME GEORGE AND HAROLD GET CAUGHT PLAYING PRANKS (AND ALSO THE RARE TIMES WHEN THEY AREN'T RESPONSIBLE FOR MISCHIEF), THEY GET CALLED INTO MR. KRUPP'S OFFICE.

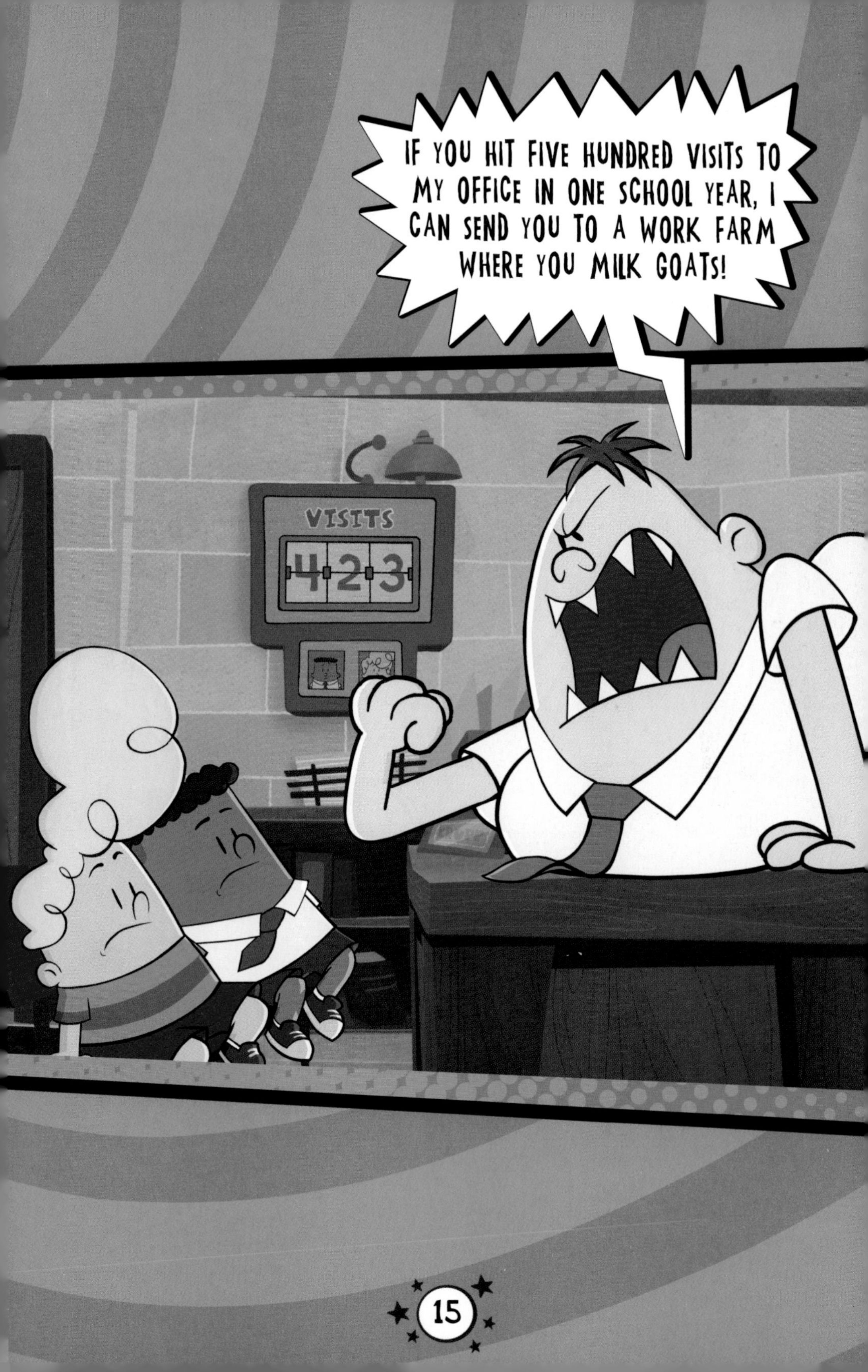
IF YOU HIT FIVE HUNDRED VISITS TO MY OFFICE IN ONE SCHOOL YEAR, I CAN SEND YOU TO A WORK FARM WHERE YOU MILK GOATS!
VISITS
423

WE HAVE A NOTE FROM A DOCTOR.
THAT NOTE IS FROM A VET!
HOPE DIES HERE

My dogs hurt. I felt eel.
I was catatonic. My throat was horse.

CHAPTER FOUR:

TREE HOUSE COMIX, INC.

WHENEVER THEY'RE NOT PLAYING PRANKS ON PRINCIPAL KRUPP, GEORGE AND HAROLD SPEND THEIR FREE TIME HANGING OUT IN THE WORLD HEADQUARTERS OF TREE HOUSE COMIX, INC. (AKA THE TREE HOUSE IN GEORGE'S BACKYARD).

INSIDE THE TREE HOUSE, THE TWO FRIENDS HAVE CREATED HUNDREDS OF COMICS STARRING SOME OF THE MOST AMAZING SUPERHEROES AND VILLAINS OF ALL TIME.

THE WORLD HEADQUARTERS OF TREE HOUSE COMIX, INC.

George writes all of the stories.
Harold illustrates them.

GEORGE AND HAROLD LOVE TO MAKE PEOPLE LAUGH. AND NOTHING MAKES PEOPLE LAUGH LIKE COMICS. WHENEVER THE TWO PALS WANT TO FIGURE OUT A FUNNY WAY TO DEAL WITH ANNOYING TEACHERS OR OTHER SILLY STUFF, THEY CREATE A NEW COMIC TO SOLVE ALL THEIR PROBLEMS IN A HILARIOUS WAY.

SOME OF THEIR GREATEST HITS INCLUDE:
CAPTAIN UNDERPANTS AND THE DREADFUL DEBACLE of DJ DROWSY DRAWERS
DJ DROWSY
BY GEORGE BEARD AN
CAPTAIN UNDERPANTS AND THE BLISTERING BLASTS OF THE BOOMING BUTTPOCOLYPSE!
TSSS
TSSSS
TSSS
CAPTAIN UNDERPANTS and the SINISTER FRIGHTS OF SCARICA FANG
story by GEORGE BEARD
pictures by Harold Hutchins
CAPTAIN UNDERPANTS and the FRENZIED FARTS OF FANNY FLAB-ULOUS
story by GEORGE BEARD
PITCHERS BY HAROLD HUTCHINS
By George Beard and Harold Hutchins

THEIR COMIC BOOKS ARE ALWAYS A HIT WITH THE OTHER KIDS . . . KIND OF LIKE FREE DONUTS OR A THREE-DOLLAR BIRTHDAY CHECK FROM AUNT CORNELIA.

George and Harold have made hundreds of hit comics. But everyone knows that their most important creation is the greatest superhero of all time . . .

. . . THE ONE AND ONLY

CHAPTER FIVE:

The Origin of CAPTAIN UNDERPANTS

Get this: Captain Underpants is *real.*

HOW EXACTLY DID THIS CRIME-FIGHTING SUPERHERO LEAP OUT OF GEORGE AND HAROLD'S COMIC BOOKS AND COME TO LIFE? WELL, IT'S SIMPLE.

AFTER LISTENING TO MR. KRUPP YELL AT THEM ONE TOO MANY TIMES, GEORGE AND HAROLD DECIDED TO HAVE SOME FUN WITH THEIR CRANKY OLD PRINCIPAL.

USING A 3-D HYPNO-RING,
THEY HYPNOTIZED MR. KRUPP.
AT FIRST, THE BOYS JUST MADE HIM DANCE AND HAD A BLAST WATCHING THEIR PRINCIPAL LOOK SILLY. BUT THEN, THEY ACCIDENTALLY (KINDA ON PURPOSE) MADE HIM BELIEVE THAT HE WAS THEIR ORIGINAL SUPERHERO CREATION: CAPTAIN UNDERPANTS.

THIS TIGHTY-WHITEY-CLAD CRIME FIGHTER APPEARS WHENEVER ANYONE SNAPS HIS OR HER FINGERS. WHEN HE GETS SPLASHED WITH WATER, HE TURNS BACK INTO PRINCIPAL KRUPP.

TRA-LA-LAAAAA!

YES, THAT'S RIGHT! WITH ONE SIMPLE SNAP OF THEIR FINGERS, ALL OF GEORGE AND HAROLD'S PROBLEMS WITH MR. KRUPP DISAPPEAR!

SNAP!
AND CAPTAIN UNDERPANTS APPEARS.
I wear pre-shrunk cotton and they call me Cap U,
Gonna bring the noise and turn your song against you!

WITH A SNAP HE'S THE CAPTAIN
NOT THE BRIGHTEST MAN
AND DON'T FORGET

WHEN HE GETS WET
YOU'RE BACK WHERE
YOU BEGAN
(BLAH BLAH BLAH)

PUT IT ALL TOGETHER

WHAT COULD POSSIBLY GO WRONG?!

CHAPTER SIX: MELVIN SNEEDLY and HIS INVENTIONS

But what would school be without a kid nemesis? Do you see that kid right there in the middle of the front row? That's Melvin Sneedly . . . homework lover, inventor, and occasional butt of George and Harold's jokes and pranks.

Melvin Sneedly is very smart. He's also a grumpy, grade-grubbing tattletale.

Time is running out and we've yet to be assigned homework!

MELVIN'S GREATEST INVENTIONS

From a young age, Melvin Sneedly displayed great talent at designing and building contraptions beyond the reach of modern science. A few of his best inventions have been useful during George and Harold's pranks. Plus, Melvin's creations have also come in handy — or caused serious problems! — when villains are on the loose in Piqua.

The PumpItUpinator 2000:
For a better body

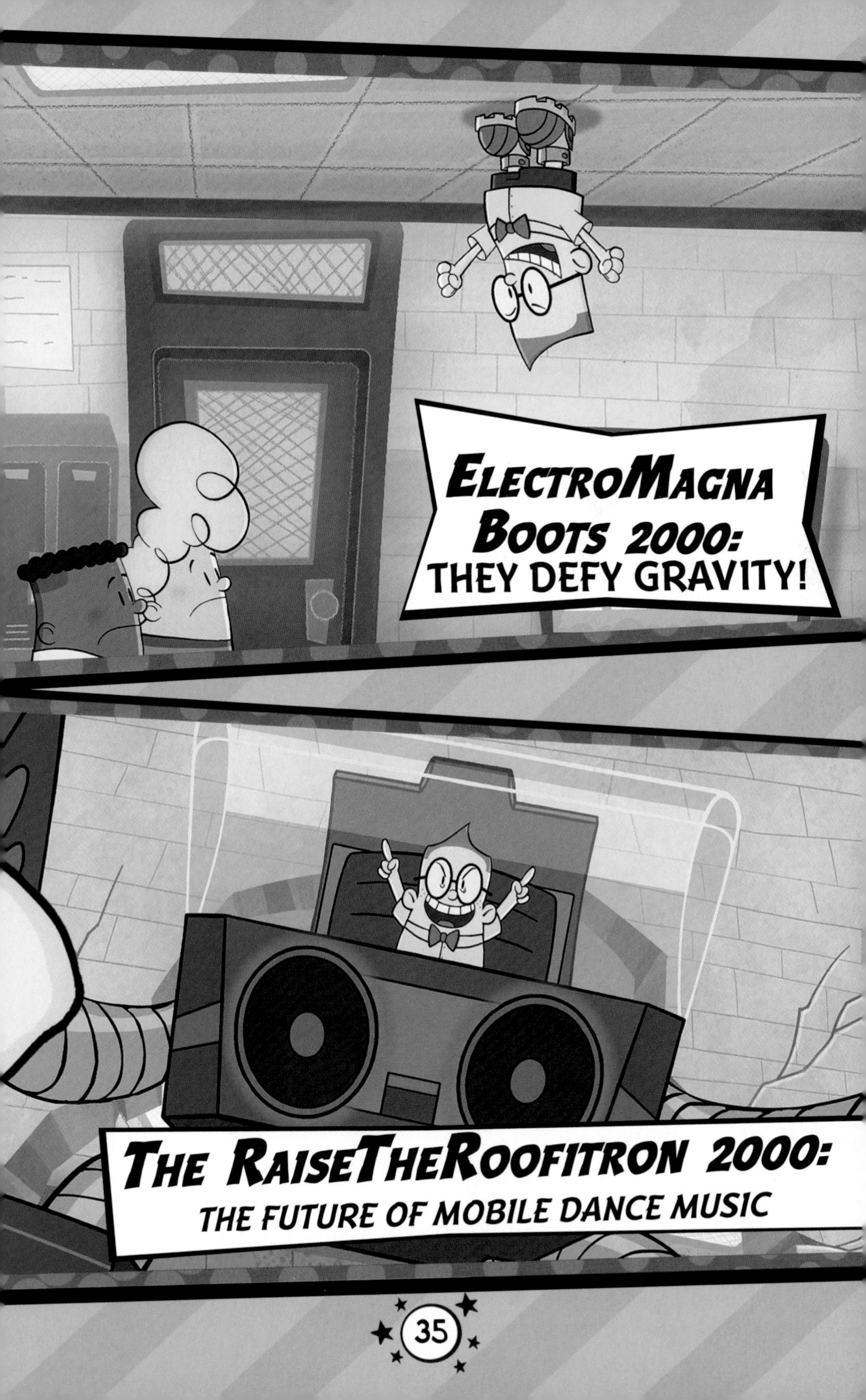
ELECTROMAGNA BOOTS 2000:
THEY DEFY GRAVITY!
THE RAISETHEROOFITRON 2000:
THE FUTURE OF MOBILE DANCE MUSIC

We're gonna go back in time to when homework was invented and stop it before it starts. It's that easy!

THE TIME TOAD 2000:

AN AMAZINGLY SOPHISTICATED PIECE OF TIME-TRAVEL TECHNOLOGY . . . POWERED BY PEANUT BUTTER.

THE PITACLE ACCELERATOR 2000:

All I have to do is win Avocadgrow and I'll get into Eliteanati Academy. Then the world will know my name: Melvin Sneedly. They will sing it!

THIS SNAZZY TOOL WAS DESIGNED TO HELP MELVIN WIN FIRST PRIZE IN THE SCHOOL'S AVOCADGROW COMPETITION.

CHAPTER SEVEN: The ZANY KIDS of JEROME HORWITZ ELEMENTARY

(besides George and Harold)

JESSICA GORDON
THE SOPHIES

ERICA WANG

ERICA IS EDITOR IN CHIEF OF THE *JEROME HORWITZ EXAMINER*, LEAD SOPRANO OF THE SCIENCE SINGERS, FORMER PRESIDENT OF THE FUTURE PRESIDENTS' CLUB . . .

George and Harold, all your girl characters just cry, shop, and brush pony hair. How 'bout a girl with dimension?

. . . AND THE LOVE OF MELVIN SNEEDLY'S LIFE.

Our brains belong together. Two brains. Thinking as one. Erica and I, a hive mind of love.

JESSICA GORDON
JESSICA IS FOCUSED ON ONE THING, AND ONE THING ALONE: HER AMAZING, GRAVITY-DEFYING HAIR.
Don't ruin my har!
THE SOPHIES
JESSICA'S SIDEKICKS (THAT'S ALL YOU NEED TO KNOW ABOUT THEM).

DRESSY KILLMAN

I hate food fights!

THIS FASHIONABLE FOURTH GRADER LOVES NOTHING MORE THAN SINGING AND TWIRLING HER WAY THROUGH THE DAY. SHE DESPISES PRANKS AND MISCHIEF AND EVERYTHING ELSE ANNOYING AND MESSY.

I grow all sorts of things in my pits. Ha-ha!

STANLEY PEET

HE'S SO SWEATY HE LEAVES A SLIPPERY TRAIL BEHIND HIM.

BO HWEEMUTH

BO IS A GIFTED SCULPTOR . . . AND DEFINITELY NOT JUST THE SCARY KID KRUPP HAS ALWAYS MADE HIM OUT TO BE.

CHAPTER EIGHT:
The STRANGE STAFF of JEROME HORWITZ ELEMENTARY

MISS ANTHROPE
THE ABSENTMINDED SCHOOL SECRETARY

I VERY MUCH NEED SOME TIME OFF.

MS. HURD

THE ANCIENT, CRANKY MUSIC TEACHER (AKA DROOPY DRAWERS . . . FOR A GOOD REASON).

DID YOU KNOW . . .

THAT MS. HURD IS SO PETRIFIED OF WEREWOLVES THROWING UP THAT SHE ONCE STAYED IN HER BASEMENT FOR THREE DAYS TO AVOID THEM?

I SURVIVED BY EATING MY OWN EYELASHES AND TOENAIL CLIPPINGS!

MS. RIBBLE

THE WORLD'S MOST BORING LANGUAGE ARTS TEACHER. MOST KIDS SPEND THEIR TIME IN HER CLASS READING GEORGE AND HAROLD'S LATEST COMIC.

I WANT A TEN-THOUSAND-WORD REPORT ON FUN . . . AND WHY IT'S WRONG.

SEÑOR CITIZEN

THE SPANISH TEACHER WHO DOESN'T SPEAK SPANISH. HE GOT HIS JOB BECAUSE MR. KRUPP WILL HIRE *ANYONE* TO BE A TEACHER. ANYONE. EVEN WORSE, THE GUY WEARS JEAN SHORTS (AKA JORTS).

JORTS!

MR. MEANER

A GYM TEACHER ON A QUEST TO MAKE GYM CLASS EVEN WORSE THAN IT ALREADY IS.

IF YOU FLABS WANT TO PASS PE, YOU WILL NEED TO MOVE THE SCALE TO "PASS PE." IF YOU ARE UNABLE TO DO SO, YOU COULD REPEAT GYM FOR UP TO TWENTY-TWO YEARS.

THIS IS BRUNHILDA, THE DISGUSTING COUCH THAT LIVES INSIDE MR. MEANER'S GYM. BRUNHILDA IS *VERY* HEAVY AND HAS BEEN A MAJOR PROBLEM FOR STUDENTS SINCE FOREVER. SOME SAY BRUNHILDA CONTAINS THE MUMMIFIED BODIES OF JEROME HORWITZ ELEMENTARY'S LAST NINETY-FIVE GYM TEACHERS. OTHERS SAY IT'S JUST FULL OF COINS (WHICH IT IS).

BRUNHILDA

MR. FYDE

THIS AWFUL SCIENCE TEACHER SPENT SIX MONTHS RESTING IN THE PIQUA VALLEY HOME FOR THE REALITY-CHALLENGED. BUT HE'S BETTER NOW, AND READY TO TEACH SCIENCE AGAIN . . . AS LONG AS EVERYONE KEEPS THE NOISE DOWN.

MS. YEWH

THE SCHOOL'S NEW FRENCH TEACHER LOVES EVERYTHING FRENCH AND HAS ALWAYS WANTED TO GO TO PARIS. BUT SHE'D SETTLE FOR FRENCH-SPEAKING CANADA.

OOH LA LA!
MS. YEWH IS AN EXCELLENT TEACHER WITH A GREAT HEAD OF HAIR AND SHE SMELLS LIKE ST. PATRICK'S DAY.
LE SIGH!

MR. REE

THE SCHOOL'S JANITOR IS A DEDICATED EMPLOYEE . . . WHO DEFINITELY DOESN'T HAVE A SECRET PAST. (OOPS, I'VE SAID TOO MUCH!) HE WORKS AT THE SCHOOL BECAUSE HE GETS TO KEEP ANYTHING THAT'S BEEN LEFT IN THE LOST AND FOUND FOR MORE THAN A MONTH.

THREE-PLY, QUILTED, PLUSH-WEAVE TOILET PAPER. NOT THE USUAL SANDPAPER YOU ORDER, MR. KRUPP. WHAT'S THE OCCASION?

IN CASE YOU'RE CURIOUS: MR. REE USED TO BE A SECRET TOILET AGENT. THE GOVERNMENT HIRED HIM TO MAKE T.E.R.D.S.–TOILET ELIMINATOR OF REALLY DANGEROUS STUFF. T.E.R.D.S. WAS A HUGE, MASSIVE TOILET CREATED TO ELIMINATE THE MOST SERIOUS THREATS ON EARTH: POISONOUS CHEMICALS, WEAPONS OF MASS DESTRUCTION, ENVELOPES . . .

MR. RECTED

THIS MELLOW MATH TEACHER IS NEVER SEEN WITHOUT HIS BOW TIE. MR. RECTED ENJOYS THE SIMPLE THINGS IN LIFE: FRESHLY DRIED SOCKS, THE BROWNIES SERVED IN THE CAFETERIA ON THURSDAYS, AND AVOIDING CONFRONTATION AT ALL COSTS.

LUNCH LADIES

THEY MAKE AWFUL FOOD THAT IS TERRIFYING. ENOUGH SAID.

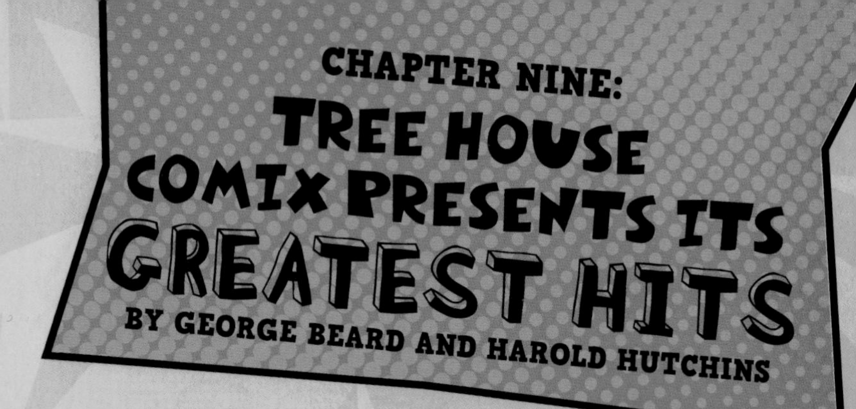

CHAPTER NINE: TREE HOUSE COMIX PRESENTS ITS GREATEST HITS

BY GEORGE BEARD AND HAROLD HUTCHINS

THE VILLAINS IN GEORGE AND HAROLD'S COMIC BOOKS HAVE BEEN KNOWN TO COME TO LIFE. (TRUST ME, IT HAPPENS FAR, FAR TOO OFTEN.)

IN THEIR QUEST TO FIND WAYS TO . . .

- **Make the school dance more exciting!**
- **Get rid of homework forever!**
- **Create a cool, kick-butt female character!**
- **(And other stuff like that)**

. . . GEORGE AND HAROLD HAVE DEVELOPED SOME OF THE COOLEST SUPER-VILLAINS IN HISTORY.

BUT AS SOON AS EACH COMIC IS FINISHED, THE BAD GUYS IN THE STORY COME TO LIFE . . . AND CAPTAIN UNDERPANTS MUST FIGHT A REAL-LIFE FOE!

George Beard
Harold Hutchins
TREE HOUSE COMIX
INC.
Read on to meet some of Tree House Comix's most exciting creations . . .

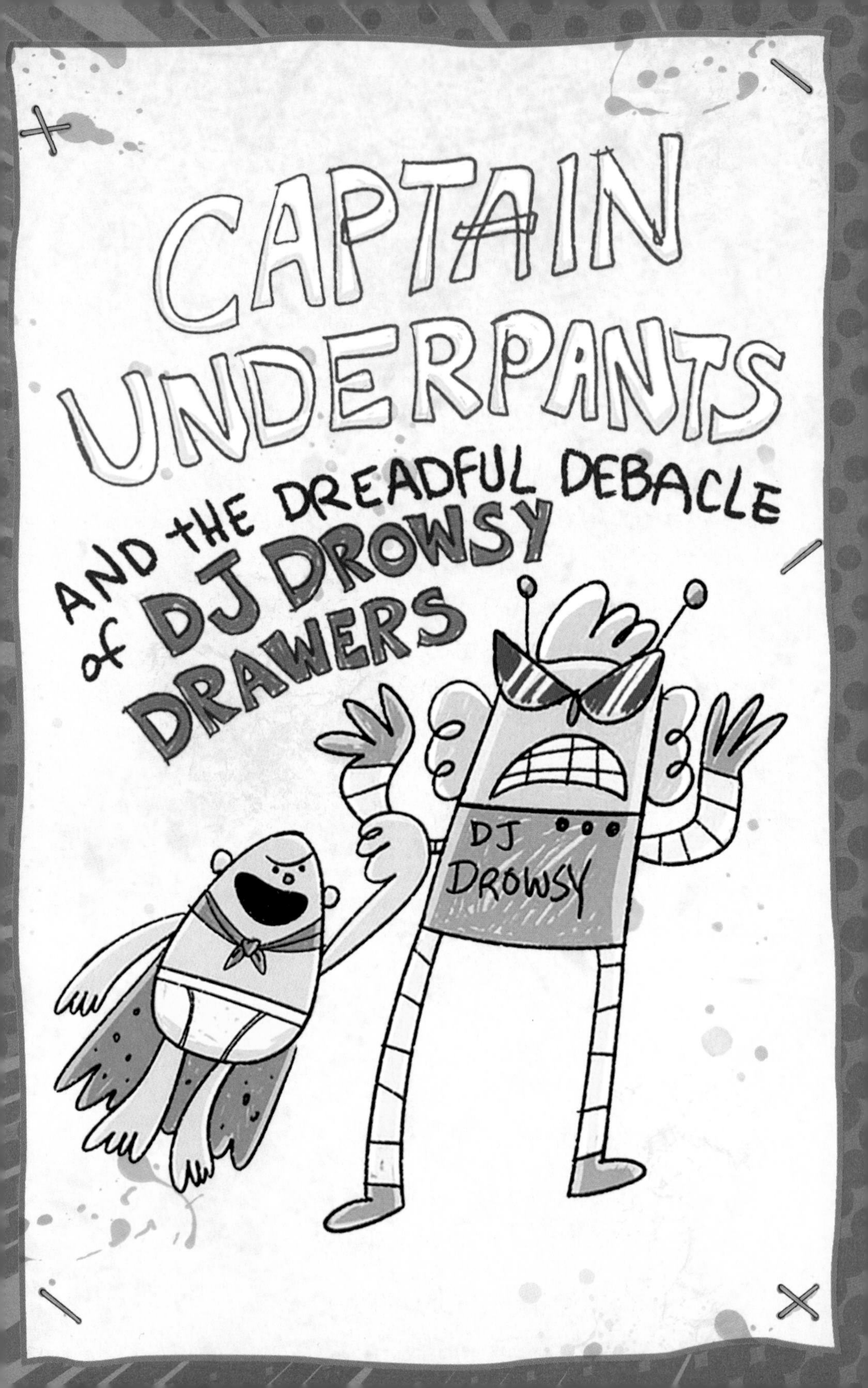
CAPTAIN UNDERPANTS
AND THE DREADFUL DEBACLE
of DJ DROWSY DRAWERS
DJ DROWSY

YAY!!
SCHOOL DANCE SOON!
DANCE
HERE
YAY!
YAY!
NOT HERE
Once upon a time, our school was gonna have a dance. All the kids were excited because they loved dancing.
But the mean principal hated dancing.
NO SHAKING!
BUTTS ARE FOR SITTING, NOT SHAKING!
I'LL RUIN THE DANCE BY HIRING THE MOST BORING DJ IN THE PHONE BOOK.
He says, "DJ Drowsy Drawers? You're hired!"
DJ
But it was a trap! DJ Drowsy Drawers was an evil alien robot lady!
BAHAHAA!!*
HAHAA!
DJ
*EVIL LAUGH

At the dance, DJ Drowsy Drawers played boring beats and did boring rap.
ZZZZ ZZZZ ZZZZ
SLEEP
BORING MUSIC
MINE
YOU'RE GETTING VERY SLEEPY! MY FLUTES'LL MAKE YOU YAWN AND MY HARPS'LL MAKE YOU SNORE!
The kids tried to dance, but they couldn't stay awake.
YAWN.
ZZZZZZ
Just then, Captain Underpants swooped in.
RAFFLE
I HEAR THERE'S A RAFFLE FOR WALKIE-TALKIES!
GULP! GULP
SODA
And he drank a whole bunch of soda!

But then Captain Underpants saw that DJ Drowsy Drawers had sleep-attacked everyone!
DJ
YOU'RE NEXT, UNDYPANTS!
DJ
But Captain Underpants fought back—for truth, justice . . .
TRUTH
JUSTICE
. . . and he kinda wanted those walkie-talkies.

So he stuffed his ears with pre-shrunk cotton.
NOW I CAN'T HEAR YOU! HERE'S YOUR WAKE-UP CALL— IT'S PUNCH O'CLOCK!
DJ
DJ
DJ Drowsy Drawers swung back . . .
. . . and knocked Captain Underpants to the bottom of the page — right next to the walkie-talkies.

Captain Underpants turned up the volume on one walkie-talkie all the way. Then he threw it at DJ Drowsy Drawers, who caught it!

Then Captain Underpants took his and burped into it.

It was so loud that all the nuts and bolts popped out of DJ Drowsy Drawers. She fell to the ground in pieces.

"Hooray!" yelled everyone who was asleep. And then they all learned the Underpants Dance.

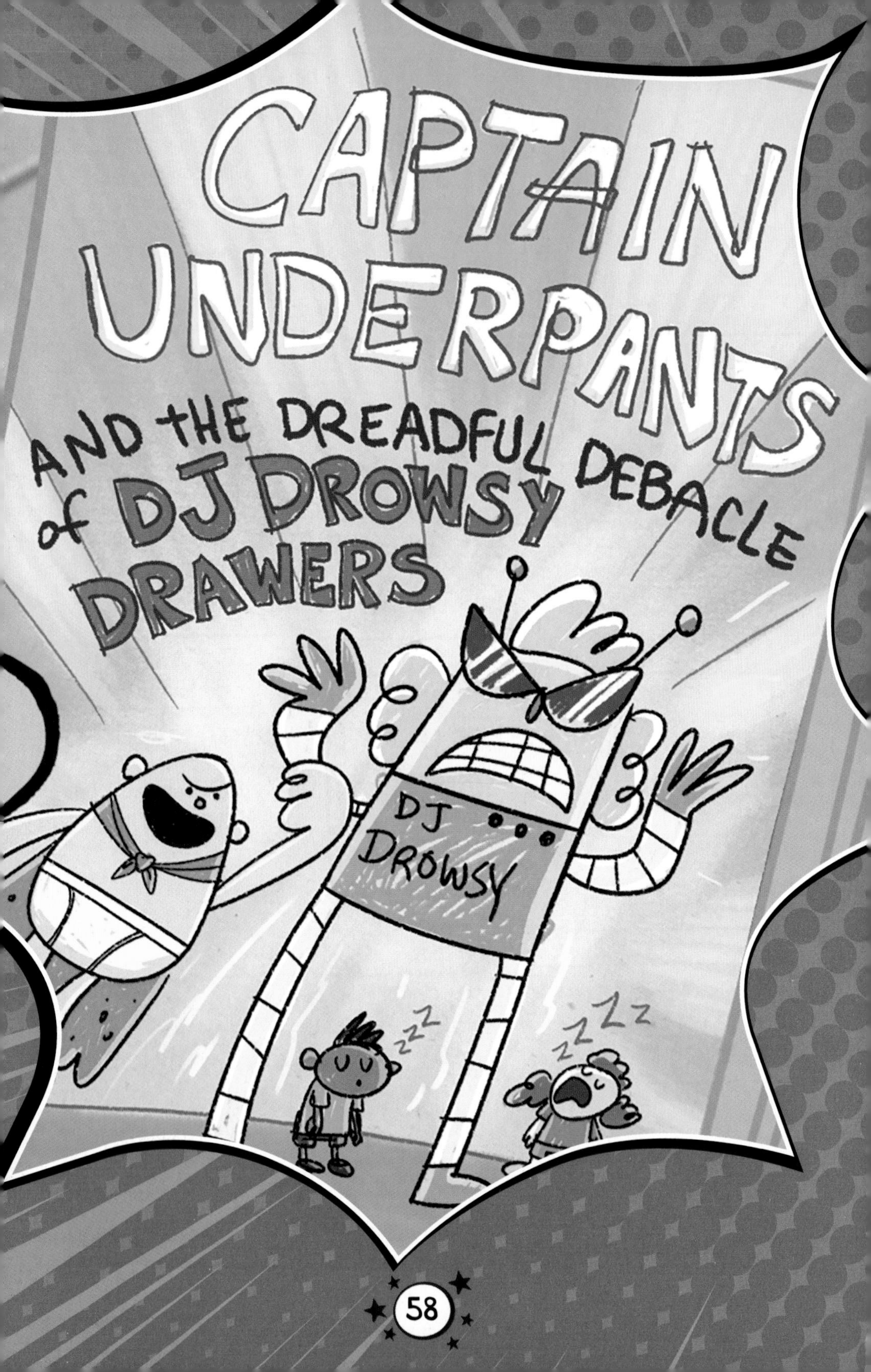
CAPTAIN UNDERPANTS
AND THE DREADFUL DEBACLE of DJ DROWSY DRAWERS
DJ DROWSY
ZZZ
ZZZZ

SO HOW, EXACTLY, DID BORING MS. HURD GO FROM DROOPY-PANTS MUSIC TEACHER TO REAL-WORLD VILLAIN WHO WREAKED HAVOC ON THE SCHOOL DANCE?

DJ Drowsy Drawers is real?!!? **And here?!!?** **How'd that happen?**

WELL, A CHEMICAL . . . ER, CAFETERIA FOOD TRUCK WAS SPEEDING TOWARD THE SCHOOL TO DELIVER NEXT WEEK'S MENU . . . AND THE TOXIC SUBSTANCE SPILLED OUT AND TURNED MS. HURD INTO DJ DROWSY DRAWERS!

SLEEEEEP! DEEEEEEP!

LUCKILY, GEORGE AND HAROLD WERE ABLE TO USE MELVIN'S RAISETHEROOFITRON 2000 AND THEIR TRUSTY SUPERHERO – GOOD OL' CAPTAIN UNDERPANTS – TO SAVE THE SCHOOL FROM EVIL!
Wake up and fight!
I don't wanna wake up and fight!

SLEEP FIGHT!

CAPTAIN UNDERPANTS AND George + Harold
the HEROIC HAMMERING
of the HOMEWORK-HEADED
HORROR!

Once there were these cool and super-buff guys, George and Harold, who did not like homework at all.
Neither did any of the other kids . . .
Homework Line Here
So the very buff guys went back in time to stop homework from being made up in the first place.

They landed in ancient Egypt right in front of a pyramid — home of the god of homework!
WE ARE HERE TO MAKE YOU UNDO HOMEWORK AND JUNK!
NUH-UH! IT'S MY THING.
And then the god of homework turned into a hydra monster with a bunch of heads.

The Homework Hydra started to eat them.

Luckily, Captain Underpants was also in ancient Egypt on vacation. He got lost looking for the bathroom.

Buff George and Buff Harold were like, "Help and stuff! Help and stuff!"

Captain Underpants zoomed up and punched the Hydra.

He dropped Buff George and Buff Harold, who were all happy.

The Hydra reached for Buff George and Buff Harold, but Captain Underpants grabbed them just in time!
Everything smashed together, and the Hydra got knocked out.
BLAM!
KO!
BLAM!

When he woke up, he couldn't remember anything — including that he'd ever thought up the idea of homework. So he didn't invent homework after all!
YAY! WE ARE THE WINNERS!
I STILL NEED A BATHROOM! TRA-LA-OOPS!
THE END

CAPTAIN UNDERPANTS and the Horrible Hostilities of the Homework Hydra

So how did the Homework Hydra spring out of the pages of George and Harold's comic book and into the lives of the students at Jerome Horwitz Elementary? Well . . . it all began because every teacher at school drooled about homework. They loved to make students miserable.

LET'S SPOIL *ALL* THEIR FREE TIME!

SO GEORGE AND HAROLD CAME UP WITH A PLAN TO GET RID OF HOMEWORK – FOREVER. BUT THINGS WENT A LITTLE WRONG . . . AND THEY TURNED THEIR TEACHERS INTO A HORRIFYING, FIVE-HEADED HOMEWORK HYDRA! (WELL, TECHNICALLY, IT WASN'T MR. MEANER'S HEAD – IT WAS HIS BUTT.)
Never fear, pre-shrunk cotton is here!
BUT FORTUNATELY, CAPTAIN UNDERPANTS CAME TO THE RESCUE!

CAPTAIN UNDERPANTS
and the
SINISTER FRIGHTS
OF
SCARICA FANG
story by GEORGE BEARD
PICTURES by Harold Hutchins

Once there was this strong female character named Scarica Fang.
She was a real know-it-all who sucked the joy out of everything. She was all "You're so wrong"
. . . and "You eat too much cheese and stuff."
Then one time this bat flew into the school and she goes, "You don't fly right."

The bat got all sad and cried — and then he bit her. He had melancholy bat venom!
And it turned her into a vimpire! Which is like a vampire, but it sucks vim, aka joy, instead of blood!
I'M SCARICA FANG. I'M SO SAD AND VANT TO SUCK YOUR JOY!
So she flew all around school biting funny bones and sucking joy!

She got bigger and stronger until she busted out of the school.
I GOT UNDERWEAR DOWN THERE! AND AN ALBINO GATOR!
Just then, Captain Underpants was leaving the Underground Underwearhouse.
I TOOK THEIR JOY, AND I WILL TAKE YOURS!
But the kids were crying and stuff.
NUH-UH! STOP IT OR ELSE!
OR ELSE NOTHING!

Captain Underpants didn't want to drop all his new underwear.
So he threw the albino gator at her, but it just stuck to her head.
IT'S ALL CLEAN AND FRESH!
YOUR ALBINO GATOR IS USELESS AGAINST ME!
So he threw all his new underwear at her.
NINJA-STYLE!

Scarica looked like an Underwear Snowman. The kids thought it was so funny they LOL'ed like crazy.
Captain Underpants was getting their joy back!
There was so much laughing that Scarica laughed, too!
STOP! HA-HA-HA, MY JOY TANK IS FILLING TOO FAST!
Scarica got so big and round, the kids could jump on her like a bouncy house all day.
TRA-LA-LAAAAA! THE END.

CAPTAIN UNDERPANTS AND THE VEXING VILLAINY OF THE VILE VIMPIRE

SO HOW DID THE VILE VIMPIRE SPRING OUT OF THE PAGES OF GEORGE AND HAROLD'S COMIC AND INTO REAL LIFE AT JEROME HORWITZ ELEMENTARY? WELL, AFTER GEORGE AND HAROLD DECIDED TO MAKE A COMIC THAT WAS A LITTLE DIFFERENT THAN USUAL . . .

Let's make a comic *about* Erica! We'll make her the star of the comic! And we'll give her special Erica powers!

. . . THINGS WENT WRONG AS USUAL. ERICA HATED THE COMIC BOOK — AND SO DID ALL THE OTHER KIDS. AND THEN MELVIN DECIDED TO TEST HIS BLISSKRIEG 2000 ON JESSICA GORDON. WHEN HE ZAPPED HER, HE ACCIDENTALLY TURNED JESSICA INTO A *REAL* VIMPIRE WHO SUCKED THE JOY OUT OF EVERYONE AROUND HER!

CAPTAIN UNDERPANTS
and the
FRENZIED FARTS
of
FANNY FLAB-ULOUS
Story by GEORGE BEARD
PITCHERS BY HAROLD HUTCHINS

Once there was a skinny guy named Fanny. But he had a huge butt, and he loved it.
He thought people with small butts were missing out.
NO, YOU'RE MISSING OUT.
WE'RE HAVING LOTSA FUN.
Even though Fanny was happy with his big butt, people made fun of him. They called him "Fanny Flabulous."
FANNY FLAB-ULOUS!
He liked that name and even got T-shirts made. But nobody bought them.
FANNY FLAB-U-LOUS
FANNY FLAB-ULOUS
SAYLE
TE-SHIRts

That made him really mad, so he went around town and crushed all the T-shirt stores.
HAT MADE HIM REALLY MAD
NOTE
FANN BOUNC
Then he crushed Captain Underpants's favorite underwear store.
But guess who was inside the store? Captain Underpants!
YOU CAN'T CRUSH BUILDINGS! ESPECIALLY UNDERWEAR STORES!
YES I CAN!
Captain Underpants tried to fight him, but he couldn't get past Fanny's big butt.

Captain Underpants pulled an extra pair of underwear from his utility waistband.

So he looked for something bigger to give Fanny Flabulous a wedgie.

Luckily, there was an underwear factory nearby. Its flagpole had a huge pair of underwear.

Captain Underpants was about to grab the underwear when Fanny made a big fart.

Captain Underpants flew back to try again, but Fanny blasted him right through the panels of the comic book!
Fanny didn't see him enter the next page . . .
. . . and Captain Underpants stuck Fanny in a huge smokestack on the factory!
CAP FLIES
CAP DROPS FANNY

Fanny couldn't stop his fart. Finally . . .

. . . he launched into space and flew all the way to Uranus, where the aliens loved big butts and Fanny's was the biggest.

He was like a king, and so he stayed there. The end.

CAPTAIN UNDERPANTS AND THE FRENZIED FARTS OF FANNY FLABULOUS

NOW, I BET YOU'RE WONDERING HOW A COMIC-BOOK VILLAIN LIKE FANNY FLABULOUS ENDED UP COMING TO LIFE AND ATTACKING THE TOWN OF PIQUA. IT ALL STARTED WHEN GEORGE AND HAROLD DECIDED TO GET BACK AT THEIR HORRIBLE GYM TEACHER, MR. MEANER, BY WRITING HIM INTO A COMIC BOOK . . .

A FEW DAYS LATER, MR. MEANER ACCIDENTALLY GOT BLASTED BY MELVIN'S PUMPITUPINATOR 2000 — AND FANNY FLABULOUS WAS BORN!

Why does he have that scary laugh?

He's a gym teacher.

(AT THIS POINT, YOU MAY WISH TO TURN DOWN THE SMELL IN THIS BOOK.)
Get ready to be Fanny-caked!
Pfffffffffffft!
I must summon my WEDGIE POWER to defeat this villain!

Luckily, Jessica Gordon, whose hair had never done anything for anyone except Jessica Gordon, became a major player in this story. Her hair was huge (thanks to Melvin's PumpItUpinator!), and it provided a soft, strong, and safe landing for Captain Underpants!

CAPTAIN UNDERPANTS
and the
QUARRELSOME TYRANNY
of
QUEEN TOOTENFARTI
Once there was this annoying French teacher who was awful and really loved French stuff and made all the kids talk French.
OUI OUI!
CLUB
YAY!
YAY!
One day she took the kids on a field trip in a bus and stuff.

They were all "Yay!" until they found out it was to a museum to see French junk.

But first, they had to walk through the mummy exhibit. The mummy was Queen Tootenfarti, an ancient Egyptian queen.

The sign said DON'T TOUCH THE MUMMY!!, but the teacher did anyway . . .

. . . and the mummy woke up and farted her mummy spirit into the teacher . . .

. . . and she made the *teacher* the mummy! Her face got all rotten and yucky.

She scared all the kids.
GROAN, GROAN!
Captain Underpants flew in.
STOP MUMMY!
I WILL EAT YOU!
I HAD TO LEAVE DINNER WITH MY MOMMY TO COME FIGHT YOU, MUMMY!
The mummy attacked, but Captain Underpants could see she was kinda sad and stuff.
10,000,000,000,000,000,000 YEARS
HEY, SHE WAS IN A BOX, LIKE, FOR A LONG TIME. SHE MUST BE LONELY!

So he wrapped himself in toilet paper and made her think he was her boyfriend.
He grabbed her hand. But she was a million years old, so it crushed to dust.
YOU'RE SO PRETTY.
GRAAR! GROAN!
OOOPS!
NOW I'M MAD AND FRENCH!
She attacked! She threw all this old stuff at Captain Underpants.

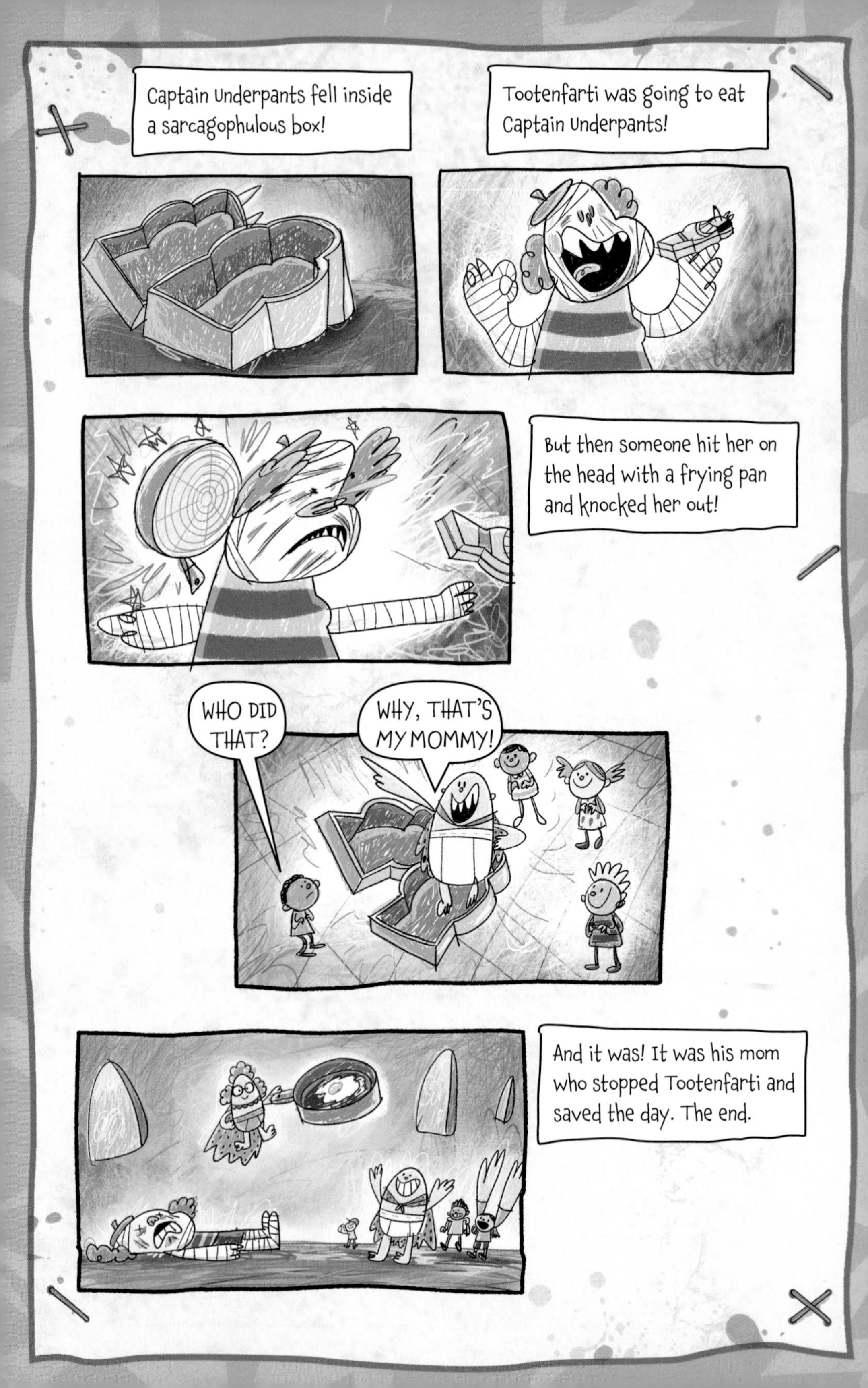
Captain Underpants fell inside a sarcagophulous box!
Tootenfarti was going to eat Captain Underpants!
But then someone hit her on the head with a frying pan and knocked her out!
WHO DID THAT?
WHY, THAT'S MY MOMMY!
And it was! It was his mom who stopped Tootenfarti and saved the day. The end.

CAPTAIN UNDERPANTS
and the Quarrelsome Tyranny of Queen Tootenfarti
SO HOW DID THE *REAL* QUEEN TOOTENFARTI END UP INVADING JEROME HORWITZ ELEMENTARY? WELL, HERE'S A GOOD ONE: WHAT DO YOU GET WHEN YOU MIX A TRUCKLOAD OF FANCY FRENCH TP AND MEGA-ULTRA-MAXIMUM-STRENGTH CLOG REMOVER WITH THE WORLD'S MOST BORING FRENCH TEACHER?
THE WHOLE JUG?!!? YOU'VE DOOMED US ALL! THAT STUFF'S EXPERIMENTAL, UNPREDICTABLE, AND KINDA PRICEY!

A TP MUMMY!
I am the queen! The queen of TP! Oui, oui, oui! I want all the TP! And once I have it, all will bow before me or never go to the bathroom again!
Hey, mummy! I'm gonna wipe you out. Get it? Cuz it's toilet paper!
AND THEN HE DID.

CHAPTER TEN:
CAPTAIN UNDERPANTS'S'S GREATEST BATTLES OF ALL TIME!!
TRA-LA-LAAAAAA!

The Squishy Predicament of Stanley Peet's Stinky Pits

NO NOOOOOOOISE! If you won't be quiet, I'll MAKE you quiet! I'll make the whole world quiet. FOREVER!

When things got out of hand during the school's Avocadgrow Competition, Melvin's Pitacle Accelerator 2000 turned noise-hating Mr. Fyde into George and Harold's latest comic book creation – **AVOCADWOE!**

Once again, the town of Piqua has one man to thank for saving them from certain doom. Captain Underpants to the rescue!

The Costly Conundrum of the CALAMITOUS CLAYLOSSUS

After loner Bo Hweemuth became friends with George and Harold, Melvin unleashed a new villain. Using his InterClaytionStation 2000, Melvin turned their huge classmate into Claylossus – a villain from George and Harold's latest comic!

BEFORE LONG, ALL OF PIQUA HAD BEEN TURNED INTO A MOUNTAIN OF CLAY – WITH CLAYLOSSUS AS ITS RULER! LUCKILY, GEORGE AND HAROLD CONVINCED MELVIN TO REVERSE THE DYNAMICAFLOB OF THE FLOOKENSPOOGER HODANK TO TURN THE INTERCLAYTIONSTATION INTO A DEINTERCLAYTIONSTATION.

ME HAVE NO FRIENDS!
Bo looks like a mountain that melted into an anger hill!
But he's still our friend. We've got to help him!

(IN NON-MELVIN TERMS: WITH CAPTAIN UNDERPANTS AND MELVIN'S HELP, GEORGE AND HAROLD WERE ABLE TO TURN CLAY BACK INTO THE SWEET, CRAFTY KID THEY HAD ALL COME TO KNOW AND LOVE.)

The Jarring Jerkiness of Judge JORTS

When Señor Citizen found a cool robe, he put it on so he could get super powers. Then things went very, very wrong . . .

The truth was, Judge Jorts was a *terrible* superhero. He caused way more problems than he solved. And just when things got bad in Piqua . . . they began to get much, much worse. That's when Captain Underpants got involved and saved the day!

WHEN A BOTTLE OF MR. KRUPP'S TOUPEE POLISH SPILLED ONTO A PILE OF DIRTY SOCKS, WELL, LET'S JUST SAY IT REALLY STANK. WHY? WELL, THE THIRD INGREDIENT IN THAT TOUPEE POLISH WAS EVIL. SO THERE YOU HAVE IT.

We gotta do something to help Captain Underpants!
Didn't Socktopus say he hates beefin' shoes?
We need a giant shoe so we can stuff him in it!
Yeah, like in our beefin' comic!

The Flustering Mindless Woe of the Flushable Memory Wipes

WHEN URINAL-CAKE SALESMAN THEODORE MURDSLY TRICKED EVERYONE AT JEROME HORWITZ INTO USING MEMORY-ERASING BUTT WIPES, HE BRAINWASHED THE WHOLE SCHOOL INTO THINKING HE WAS AMAZING . . . AND HE TRIED TO TAKE OVER THE SCHOOL!

I'LL WIPE YOUR BRAINS SO CLEAN, YOU'LL BE ABLE TO EAT OFF THEM!

Luckily, Captain Underpants saved the day . . . with a giant vat of chocolate pudding. (Obviously.)

The Soggy Salvation of the SWIRLING SWEATNAMI

WHEN GEORGE AND HAROLD TRAVELED BACK IN TIME TO TRY TO ALTER THE MOMENT IN HISTORY WHEN MR. KRUPP TURNED INTO A MEAN OLD GRUMP, THINGS DIDN'T GO QUITE THE WAY THEY'D PLANNED. AND WHEN *MELVIN* GOT INVOLVED, THINGS GOT MUCH, MUCH WORSE.

It's nothing personal. I just don't like you.
AHHHH! THERE'S NOTHING QUITE LIKE SURFING AWAY FROM BAD GUYS ON A WAVE OF SWEAT.
Grab a dolphin floaty and surf your way to freedom!
SURF'S UP!
Sweatnammiiiii!

SMARTSY FARTSY
The Sickening Fumes of the Smartsy Fartsy
MELVIN'S LATEST INVENTION, THE ELEVAPOR 2000, TURNED LIFELESS GAS INTO AN INTELLIGENT, LIVING CLOUD. SO GEORGE AND HAROLD USED IT TO MAKE GEORGE'S FART COME TO LIFE! WICKED!
Quick, before Melvin gets back, let 'er rip!

It's Smartsy Fartsy from our comic! Only smart! We made him out of my fart!
YOU CAN'T FIGHT GAS!
Oh, no! I breathed him in and I taste fart!

TOOT FAIRY
The Troublesome Treachery of the Thieving Toot Fairy

BET YOU THOUGHT IT COULDN'T GET MUCH WORSE THAN SMARTSY FARTSY, THE STINKY GAS . . . WELL, IF THAT'S THE CASE, YOU'D BE WRONG.

Hey, have you guys noticed someone sneaking into your room at night? But instead of taking teeth, they steal your farts?

That's a great idea for a comic book — thanks!

I disguised myself as the Tooth Fairy . . . but I'm really a Toot Fairy who's come to steal farts! Now I'll create a fart army! You will FEAR ME! You will give me your respect — or I will *take it* along with your farts!

SILENT . . . BUT DEADLY!

CHAPTER ELEVEN: GEORGE AND HAROLD'S CREATE-A-COMIC

This is _______________ _______________. One day, _______________ was in
(your first name) (your last name) (your first name)

_______________ class when a _______________ dude _______________ through
(school subject) (adjective) (verb ending in -ed)

the door. He cried out, "Greetings, _______________ fools! My name is Mr.
(adjective)

_______________ _______________ and I am your new teacher."
(gross adjective) (gross thing)

_______________ had seen this _______________ guy before! He was a
(your first name) (adjective)

_______________ villain who was trying to take over the _______________!
(adjective) (place)

"You're not a teacher!" _______________ shouted. "You are the evil villain,
(your first name)

Professor _______________ _______________!" _______________ grabbed a
(gross adjective) (gross thing) (your first name)

_______________ _______________ and _______________ it at their new teacher.
(adjective) (large thing) (verb ending in -ed)

But the evil villain just _______________. "You can't stop me!" he yelled. "Not
(verb ending in -ed)

even that _______________ superhero, Captain _______________ can stop me!"
(adjective) (article of clothing)

"Maybe not. But I know who can! This is a job for Captain Underpants!"

_______________ cried.
(your first name)

"*Tra-la-laaaaa!*" yelled Captain Underpants as he _______________ into the
(verb ending in -ed)

room. "I am here to save all of you and your _______________ _______________."
(adjective) (thing ending in -s)

He grabbed a _______________ and swung it at the _______________ bad guy.
(item found in a classroom) (adjective)

The evil villain _______________ to the floor. "Hooray!" shouted everyone.
(verb ending in -ed)

"_______________ and Captain Underpants saved the day again!"
(your first name)

Reminder:

A **VERB** is an action word (like *run, hop, smash, crush,* etc.)

An **ADJECTIVE** is a word that describes a person, place, or thing (like *stinky, green, slimy, gross,* etc.)